Little One

JANE GODWIN
& GABRIEL EVANS

For Sophie Mullins,
and in memory of Bubba.
J.G.

To my sister M,
because of Bluebell.
G.E.

First published by Affirm Press, 2021
This edition published by Affirm Press, 2024
Bunurong/Boon Wurrung Country
28 Thistlethwaite Street, South Melbourne, VIC 3205

1 3 5 7 9 10 8 6 4 2

A catalogue record for this book is available from the National Library of Australia

ISBN: 9781923135833 (paperback)
Cover and internal design © Affirm Press
Printed and bound in China by
RR Donnelley Asia Printing Solutions Ltd.

Ed has a teddy,
Lola has a blanket,
Penny has her Elly...

but Little One is mine.

She's soft like mist,
she's always warm.

Her eyes look
at my eyes.

We talk without
speaking.

Little One knows
everything about me.

Ed says that
Little One is all
worn out.

Lola says she's
falling apart.

'She feels empty
when I hold her,'
says Penny.
'She's dirty.'

But Little One isn't any of those things,
and she never feels empty to me.

Little One sits on my bed
and waits for me.
We look out at the world,
we wonder together.

At night-time,
Little One sings me a lullaby.

Then, in the morning,
I close the door
and go out into the day.

One day, Penny brings
her new puppy to the park.

Ed brings only himself.

I bring Little One.

And Lola's blanket stays
in the pusher.

'Her name's Mimi,'
says Penny.

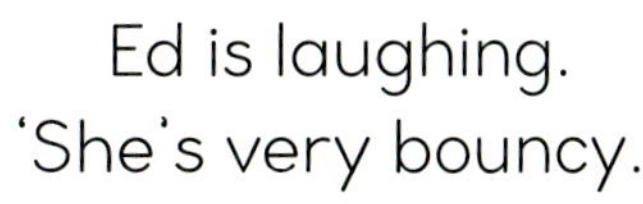

Ed is laughing.
'She's very bouncy.'

Mimi wriggles in my arms
and nips my fingers
with her tiny teeth.

It tickles!

Mimi wants Little One!

'You can't have her,' I say. 'Little One is mine.'

'Now look what you've done, Mimi!'

I put Little One up high.

Mimi's ears are the colour of chocolate ice-cream.
She has a warm, round tummy.

We take her for a walk and show her the whole park.
It's good to have a puppy to play with!

Mimi gets tired out
because she's still a baby.
I carry her all the way home.

At bedtime,
I can't find Little One.

We look
everywhere.

But we don't find her.

Ever.

I don't know where she went.

After a while,
Dad buys a new
little one.

'Is this your doll now?' Ed says.

But it scares me, because
it isn't Little One at all.

I take the piece of her dress
that Mimi had torn,
and rest it on my pillow.

It still feels soft.

Ed doesn't laugh at me.
'It's okay,' he says.
'Now you can remember her.'

And I do.

Sometimes at night-time,
I still talk to her.
I sing a lullaby.

And sometimes, in the morning,
before I go out into the day,

I imagine that I'll open the door
and Little One will be waiting...

to wonder at the world with me.